My Bumblebee and Me

Written by Sue James

Illustrated by Kathleen A. Renninger

Published in USA by Sue James

Dedicated to Ms. Sue's Crew

Nora, Eve, Joslynn, Levi, Nate, Maddie, Cooper, Carter, Viraj, Anabelle, Natalie, Brock, Chase, Madelyn, Devin, Payton, Logan and Abby.

Thank you for your inspiration; you are the reason this book was written. I will always love you.

MARCH 2023

Acknowledgements

This book was made possible because of the collaborative efforts of many talented ladies including, our editor, Jessica Brown, Illustrator, Kathleen Renninger, and with the help of Nora Dickey who loved the bumblebee story from the beginning.

Table of Contents

Chapter One

"Buzz By"

I made a strange friend the other day as I was leaving through our back gate. Bam! He got right in my face! The biggest yellow and black bumblebee I had ever seen. He buzzed there, right in front of me and I couldn't get past him.

Jokingly I said, "Mr. Bumblebee, please excuse me, but I would like to get by you!"

To my surprise he began to show off, performing what I think was a mid-air acrobatic show. He flew upside down, sideways, zig zagged and jetted around until he finally let me by.

"Weird," I said out loud and went out the gate.

This was a special day because we were headed to an amusement park and I was so excited. My hat on my head, a good pair of shoes and money in my pocket, I was free to ride all day: roller coasters, water rides and tons of food.

We stopped for breakfast along the way. As we waited for our food, I noticed a bumblebee in the doorway.

"I wonder if that's--?" I stopped. I was talking out loud without realizing it.

"What did you say?" Terry said, looking puzzled.

"Oh, nothing."

I watched people come in and out the restaurant door; the bumblebee was causing quite a commotion. He was trying to get in as people went in and out.

"Don't swat at him! He will sting you," one woman told her young son as they all tried to get into the door along with the bumblebee.

The boy continued to wave his hands around, causing the bee to fly closer to him.

Bumblebee was getting mad!

“Where are you going?” Terry asked as I jumped out of my seat and headed for the front door. “Our food is here!”

“Just a minute.”

Quickly walking across the restaurant, I hurried to open the door letting the people in and the bee out.

“Momma, he was going to sting me!” said the frightened child.

I looked out and saw the bee just at my eye level, looking at me on the other side of the glass.

Back at the table, I mumbled to Terry, “I think that‘s my bumblebee from the house.”

“I think you’re imagining things!” Terry growled. “Let’s eat. I want to get to the park.”

Chapter Two

"The Amusement Park"

It felt as if we rode for hours in the car but finally, we were there! We raced to the tram. It took so long to get to the gate. We hopped out. The first thing we did was get in line for the front car of the nearest roller coaster.

Everyone was so excited and people were screaming with joy and fear as the cars raced down the track.

I was counting how many people were in front of us, when I noticed a big bee by the sign that said, "Keep head back during launch." The bumblebee saw me at the same time because he began to fly towards me in the crowd. "Get out bee!" one of the men in line shouted, taking off his hat and trying to hit the bee.

A lady saw the bumblebee and leaned way over the rail to let him by her. He continued through the line until he stopped right in front of me. He hovered there for just a moment as if to say, “Are you sure you want to ride this thing?”

“It’s fine. I’ve been coming here since I was little,” I said to the bee. “I’ve been on this roller coaster many times before.”

Terry looked around to see who I was talking to, then said, “Liz, what are you doing?’

“Well, I think I’m talking to my bumblebee. See!” I said, pointing to the bee.

Just then the ride's train pulled up. The bee flew off and we got on the roller coaster.

"Lizzie, there is not a bumblebee here. I'm getting worried about you," Terry said as we strapped in.

I screamed and just loved every terrorizing minute of that ride.

Chapter Three

"Safety Check"

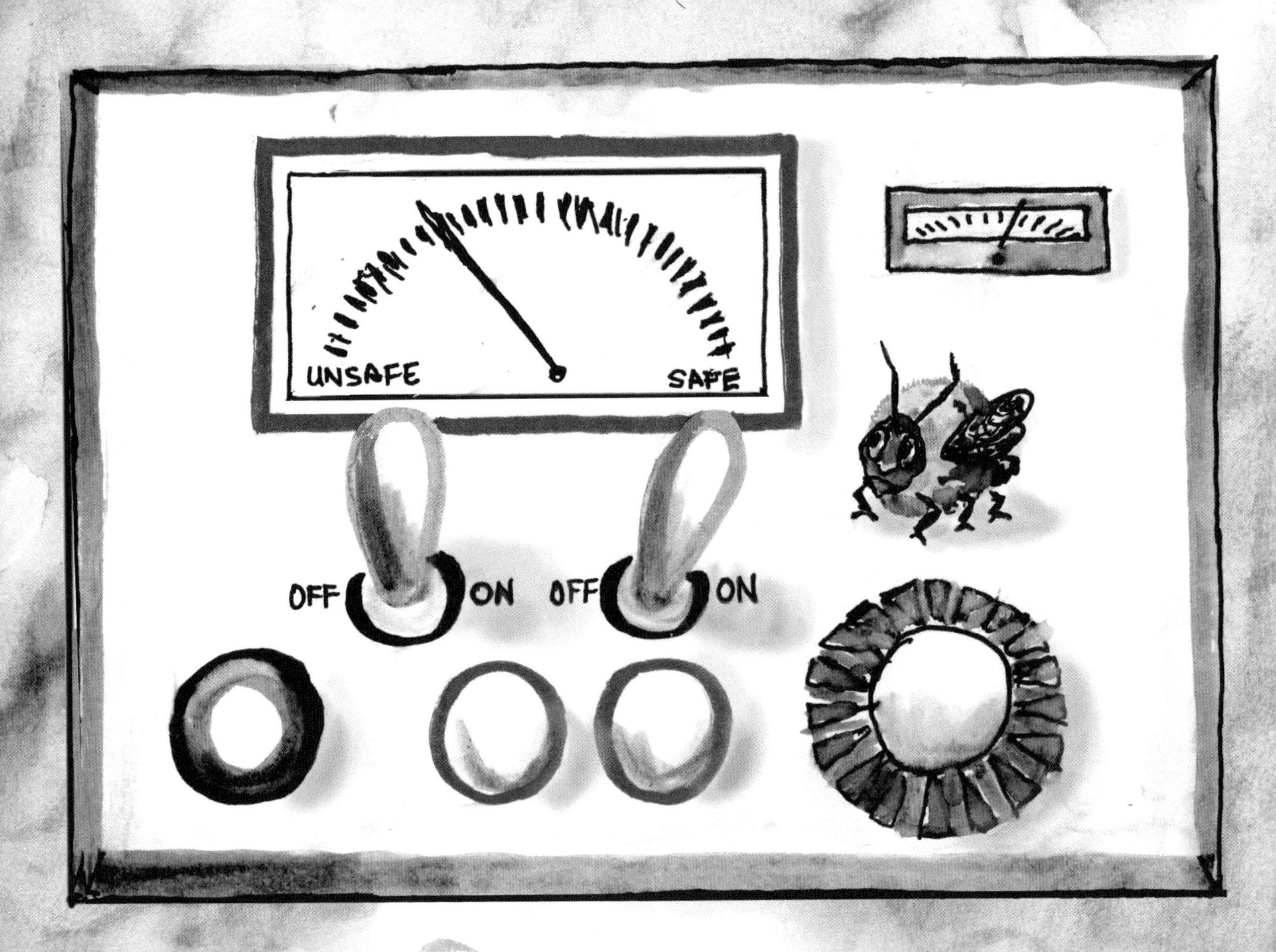

After a couple of roller coasters in a row, we decided to chill out on a slower ride like the monorail. A train was already there, so we got on right away. Terry and I sat near the front and I could see all the buttons, switches and toggles used to run the monorail. Right on the control board was a bumblebee!

"There he is again!" I said to Terry.

"What are you talking about?"

"Look at the control board," I said pointing to the bee.

"Oh, I see him. Liz, that could be ANY bumblebee. The park is full of them!"

"Well, I guess you're right."

I kept watching the bee while we waited for the rest of the people to board. I noticed that same bumblebee began to fly all around. He flew in and out of the train, near the support poles underneath the track, and back to the control panel in the car ahead of us.

When the monorail driver entered the cab, that bee aggravated him so much, the poor guy had to get out of his seat and leave the control car! Then that same bee came into our compartment and landed on the exit door.

"We just got here. It's not time to go! Why are you making trouble?" I whispered to him so Terry wouldn't hear me. "Is everything alright bumblebee?"

The bee buzzed loudly, moved his wings without flying and planted himself, vibrating on our cabin's door.

"Does he really want us to leave?" I thought to myself. The next thing we heard was an alarm ringing on the train.

Another park attendant approached the monorail and I heard him tell the operator the train wasn't working right and all the people had to get off.

"Terry, I think my bumblebee was trying to tell us something", I said as I showed him the bee on our exit door.

"Do you really think so?"

"Yes, I do."

"Folks, we have a malfunction. Please leave the train using the exit door on your right," was announced over the loud speaker."I told you he was trying to show us something. See how he is staying on our exit door? He wants us to get off!" I said to Terry frustrated that he didn't believe me.

"Well, since you two are such good friends, will you get him to move so we can leave the train?" Terry asked sarcastically.

"Don't worry bumblebee. We're getting off with everybody else." Once I told him that, he flew away.

Chapter Four

"Look Over Here"

“I’m beat.” “Me too! Let’s get out of here. I want to go home,” Terry said rubbing the back of his neck. “What a great day. We had so much fun. Did you get to ride everything you wanted?”

“Yes, I did.”

“Do you want to buy anything before we go home?” Terry asked, then slowed his walk in front of the store.

"No, I just want to visit the bathroom before we go and …AH!"

"What?"

"Bumblebee, you scared me!" I said, annoyed at him. He was stopped in front of me blocking my way again, just like this morning at the house.

Terry saw the bumblebee and said, "Lizzie, I'm starting to think this is *your* bumblebee. He's been showing up all day."

"Finally, you believe me! That's what I've been trying to tell you."

"Bumblebee, what do you want me to see?" I gently asked him now that I was calmed down.

Terry and I watched him as he slowly flew away from us to a small waterfall that had a row of rose bushes beside it and there in the middle of that beautiful sight was the biggest spider web either of us ever saw! My Bumblebee hovered over it as the web sparkled in the sun.

"It's the size of a pizza." Terry stared in amazement.

"Yeah, the threads look like spun silver and My Bumblebee showed us. Like that's pretty amazing too!"

"Thank you my dear bumblebee. You must know somehow that I love to see spider webs," I gently told the bee in appreciation.

Terry smiled at me, took my hand, and my bumblebee flew away.

"I wonder if he will be there when we get home?" I asked Terry as we walked out of the park's gate.

"I don't know."

Then we heard over the loud speaker, "The monorail is closed for repairs and will not be available to our park guests today."

"Incredible!" I said to Terry.

THE END

Bumblebee Question and Answer Sheet
www.bumblebee.org

Can bumblebees sting or bite?

Actually they can do both, but they usually do not. Their jaws, called mandibles, are not strong enough to cause any pain even if they did bite. Bumblebees rarely sting. There are reports of bumblebee stings, but only if they were roughly handled or someone is invading their nest. They are known by bee handlers as a most accommodating insect, meaning they are very easy going and usually not aggressive.

What do they eat?

Bumblebees only drink nectar and pollen. Flowers are needed for their survival. It has been estimated that a bumblebee's full honey stomach, where the bumblebee stores the nectar, will give a bumblebee about 40 minutes of flying time. Without the energy in nectar, a bumblebee cannot fly. If a bumblebee cannot fly, it cannot reach flowers to get nectar and as a result, it will die.

Do bumblebees make honey?

They do make a small amount of watery honey, but not nearly enough to harvest by humans. A successful nest will have a few teaspoons.

Why are they covered with black and yellow fuzz?

The fuzz we are seeing on the bumblebee is actually thick hair. It acts as insulation keeping the bee warm in cold weather. The colors of the bumblebee's hair act as a warning to protect it from predators.

Do bumblebees have ears?

A bumblebee does not have ears. Scientists are unsure if bumblebees can actually hear sound, but we do know that bumblebees can feel the vibrations of sounds through wood and other materials.

Why do bumblebees look like they have dots on their eyes?

Bumblebees, common with many other insects, have three ocelli known as primitive eyes arranged in a triangular pattern on the top of the head. They look like dots to us.

What can I do to help the bumblebees?

Visit www.bumblebee.org for advice on how to help the bumblebees. This website gives useful information including how to make a window box full of flowers to help feed the bees.

Some Helpful Tips:

Bumblebees need three things:

1. A continuous succession of flowers supplying nectar and pollen throughout the season.
2. A warm, sheltered place to nest that faces south.
3. A secure place for the queen to hibernate.

You can also:

Supplement nectar during the early, cold days of spring.
Help any grounded bumblebees you may discover.
Stop using insecticide sprays containing poison.

About the Author

Sue James has been a child care provider for over seventeen years. Often, she tells stories to help the children in her care understand their world. She lives in Waynesboro, Pennsylvania with her daughter, husband and three cats. This is her first children's book.

About the Illustrator

Kathleen Renninger is an artist, graphic designer, and author living with her husband in Blue Ridge Summit, Pennsylvania. She has written and illustrated her own book, "Pages from a Nature-Lover's Diary".

Made in the USA
Columbia, SC
26 October 2017